The Cockerel, the Mouse and The Little Red Hen

illustrated by Jess Stockham

Child's Play (International) Ltd
Ashworth Rd, Bridgemead, Swindon, SN5 7YD UK
Swindon   Auburn ME   Sydney
© 2005 Child's Play (International) Ltd   Printed in Heshan, China
ISBN 978-1-904550-75-4   L210411FUFT0611754
9 10 8
www.childs-play.com

Once upon a time,
a little red hen lived in a house on a hill,
with a fine white cockerel and a small dark mouse.
The house had shiny red doors and shutters.

Across the valley
on another hill lived
a family of bad-tempered foxes.
The door of their house had been
slammed so many times it was hanging off
its hinges, and two windows had been broken.

One morning, the little bad-tempered foxes
said to their bad-tempered father,
"it's not fair! We're so hungry.
We haven't eaten for days!"

"All right, all right!" shouted the bad-tempered father fox. "But I'm too tired to go far for food!"

"We could eat the little red hen across the valley," suggested one of the little foxes.

"And the fine white cockerel!" said another.

"And the small dark mouse for a snack!" joined in another little fox.

"I'll go and fetch my sack," said the bad-tempered father, and he almost smiled.

That same morning, the cockerel and the mouse
came into the kitchen as the little red hen
was making breakfast.

"Who'll get some sticks to light the fire?"
she asked. "Not me," answered the cockerel.
"Not me," said the mouse.
"Then I'll do it myself," said the little red hen.
And she did.

"Who will fill the kettle from the stream?"
asked the little red hen.
"Not me," answered the cockerel.
"Not me," said the mouse.
"Then I'll do it myself,"
said the little red hen.
And she did.

The little red hen put the kettle on to boil,
then turned to the cockerel and the mouse.
"Who will get the breakfast ready?" she asked.
"Not me," answered the cockerel.
"Not me," said the mouse.
"Then I'll do it myself," said the little red hen.
And she did.

All the way through breakfast, the cockerel
and the mouse grumbled and argued. They spilt
the milk jug, and put crumbs all over the floor.
"What a mess!" said the little red hen.
"Who will tidy everything up?"
"Not me," answered the cockerel.
"Not me," said the mouse.

"Then I'll do it myself,"
said the little red hen.
And she did.

When she had finished, she felt like sitting down,
but she still had chores to do.
"Who will help me make the beds?" she asked.
"Not me," answered the cockerel.

"Not me," said the mouse.
"Then I'll do it myself,"
said the little red hen.
And she went
upstairs at once.

After breakfast, the cockerel and the mouse
were so tired that they fell asleep. All of a sudden,
there was a knock at the door.
"Are you going to answer that?" asked the mouse.
"Not me. I'm too tired," said the cockerel.

"Why don't you?"

"Well, it might be a parcel of cheese for me," thought the mouse, so he did.

The minute he opened the door, the bad-tempered fox leapt into the house.

"Got you!" he shouted, as he popped
the mouse into his sack.
"Got you!" he shouted, as he popped
the cockerel into his sack.
The little red hen came running
downstairs to see what was the matter.
"Got you!" the fox shouted, as he popped
her into his sack, and tied it up.

"Ooooh, I wish I hadn't been so lazy!" wailed the cockerel. "Ooooh, I wish I hadn't been so grumpy!" wailed the mouse.

"Don't worry," said the little red hen.
"Everything will be fine.
I've got my sewing kit
- and a very good idea!"

The fox staggered all the way down the valley,
carrying the heavy sack. He was very hot and tired,
so before he climbed up the hill to his house,
he thought he would have a rest by the stream.
He hadn't been sitting for long, before
he fell fast asleep.

As soon as the little red hen heard him snoring,
she fetched out her scissors and snipped
a mouse-sized hole in the sack.
"Quickly!" she whispered, "go and fetch
a stone as big as yourself. Hurry!"

The mouse was soon back. "Push the stone into the sack," whispered the little red hen. Then she cut a hole in the sack as big as the cockerel. "Go and find a stone as big as yourself," she said. "Hurry!"

As soon as the cockerel returned, she told him to push the stone into the bag, also. Then she climbed out of the sack, put in a stone as big as herself, and quickly sewed up the hole.

Then all three of them ran as fast as they could
up the hill to their house, shut all the windows
and locked the door.

The bad-tempered fox, meanwhile,
remained fast asleep, until the sun began
to go down.

 "Grrh!" he grumbled. "It's cold, and I have to carry
this heavy sack all the way home. It's not fair!"

He started to cross the stream, but the sack
of stones was so heavy that he was pulled
right under the water. He could have let go
and floated to the top, but he was so greedy,
and bad-tempered at the thought of letting go
of his supper, that he held on tight, and was
never seen again.

The fine white cockerel and the small dark mouse
made the little red hen sit and rest in the most
comfortable chair, while they lit the fire,
filled the kettle, made the breakfast and did
all the other chores around the home.
And they never grumbled again, not once!